Coffee and Dreams

Volume 4

COFFEE AND DREAMS
VOLUME 4

SHORT STORIES WITH

Alinar Den & JJ Caler
Arya Anakin - Daniel Nick - J Lee Bagan

Coffee and Dreams

Volume 4

Short stories with

Alinar Den and JJ Caler

Featuring

Daniel Nick - J Lee Bagan – Arya Anakin

Published by Caler and Den Publishing

Coffee and Dreams: Volume 4

First publication, September, 2024

Copyright © 2024 Alinar Den & J.J. Caler

The Anderson Memorandum

Copyright © 2024 J.J. Caler

Written by J.J. Caler

Building the Dream

Copyright © 2024 Alinar Den

Written by Alinar Den

Root of all Evil

Copyright © 2024 Daniel Nick

Written by Daniel Nick

A Perfect Place

Copyright © 2024 Arya Anakin

Written by Arya Anakin

Chit Chat

Copyright © 2024 J Lee Bagan

Written by J Lee Bagan

Coffee and Dreams is a Trademark of Alinar Den and JJ Caler

All Rights Reserved

This is a work of fiction. Names, characters, places, and incidents either are the product of the author's imagination or are used fictitiously. Any resemblance to actual persons, living or dead, events, or locales is entirely coincidental.

All rights reserved.

No part of this book may be reproduced, distributed, or transmitted in any form or by any means, including photocopying, recording, or other electronic or mechanical methods, without the prior written permission of the author, except in the case of brief quotations embodied in critical reviews and certain other noncommercial uses permitted by copyright law.

DEDICATION

Coffee and Dreams Volume 4
To everyone who has a dream

And to Alinar, for sharing the dream.

Alinar Den & JJ Caler

Root of all Evil
For Andrew and Alice. The fight spans generations, but your family is legion. Thank you.

Daniel Nick

A Perfect Place
To JJ CALER and ALINAR; You don't always come across little people doing great things. Well, unless you meet them at the perfect time, in a perfect place...
Arya Anakin

Chit Chat
This little tidbit of literary playfulness is dedicated to the memorable
Sci-Fi rags of my long-ago youth.
Analog
Amazing Stories
Asimov's Science Fiction
Fantasy and Science Fiction

J Lee Bagan

Contents

Coffee and Dreams i
   DEDICATION vi
The Anderson Memorandum 1
   BASIC TRAINING 5
   INTO THE STORM 11
   INTO THE JUNGLE 14
   AWAKENING 17
   AWAKE 19
   THE HUT 21
   THE BOAT 25
   AWAKENED 30
A Perfect Place 35
   The Third Time 39
   The Last Time 47
   The First Time 53
Root of all Evil 65
   In The Blood 69
Chit Chat 111
   Nedha 115
Building the Dream 125
   12 129
   22 135

32	139
ABOUT THE AUTHOR	146

The Anderson Memorandum

By JJ Caler

Copyright © 2024 JJ Caler

All rights reserved.

J. J. CALER

BASIC TRAINING

In the annals of time, there are stories that echo through generations, tales of courage, sacrifice, and the unyielding human spirit. This is one such story, a memorandum of the Anderson family, where the past and present intertwine in a dance of fate and destiny.

Welcome to "The Anderson Memorandum," where the past is never truly gone, and the future is always just a heartbeat away.

"Anderson!"

"Yes, Chief Petty Officer," He answered, as he stood tense with his freshly polished boots at a forty-five.

Everyone else in the barracks was down on the floor doing push-ups. Anderson was the last man standing.

They were told that whoever passed the inspection, they would get an extra hour in the break room while the rest were doing push-ups.

"Anderson, your name is too long!"

"Yes, Chief Petty Officer," he answered loud and clear.

There were three Petty Officers making the rounds for the first inspection. Anderson had been passed by at least twice by each of them, and he thought he was home free.

"Look at the state of your locker, Anderson!"

"Aye, Aye, Chief Petty Officer," he nearly yelled back as he turned to look.

His locker was high and dry, hard and tight when this started. Each one of the inspectors had pulled his clothes out and tossed them on the floor looking for mistakes. All except that one t-shirt. They left it in place. Completely untouched until the previous Petty Officer took his turn. He pulled it out, shuffled it around and put it back.

"That t-shirt is not regulation, CumDrop!" The Chief Petty Officer snapped.

"No Sir!" Anderson yelled in acknowledgment.

"CumDrop! I am not a sir and I am in charge of renaming in this company! Do you think you are better than your company?" He barked.

"No, Petty Officer!" Anderson pulled himself tight again, standing at attention and looking directly across the room at a spot on the wall.

"Then why are you still standing up? Hit the deck and give me ten, right now!"

"Aye, aye," he shouted back as he squatted and thrust his legs out behind him.

"Count them off, CumDrop!"

"One... Two... Three..." Anderson began the count, pacing his push-ups.

"Hold that position, CumDrop!" the Chief Petty Officer ordered.

Anderson froze in mid push, his elbows still bent and the Petty Officer began walking down the line of men, looking for his next target.

Anderson looked at his bunk mate who was looking back and they both rolled their eyes and grinned before turning their faces back to the floor to hide them.

They were learning there was an unwritten rule or two in the Navy. First, you follow every order to the letter... Unless you could avoid it without being caught. That is why Anderson eased his elbows out and let himself rest on the floor, keeping all three Petty officers in his view. As soon as one looked like his head was turning toward them, he and Brad would both lift themselves off the floor into the down position.

Not everyone was picking up on it. There were a few others, but there was a silent agreement. No one said anything. They all had the impression that the Petty Officers knew exactly what they were doing, but as long as they managed it without being called out, they would look the other way.

Basic training...

It wasn't just about learning all the rules. It was about surviving all the rules. There was kind of a wink and a nod to it. The Petty Officers seemed to respect a little ingenuity in a sailor. But if you got called out, well, you messed up didn't you. And you would pay the piper twice. Not only did you break the rules but you let down your commander.

There was a lot of psychological training going on there that we didn't really pick up on until much later in life. Sleep deprivation, the way that superiors were always antagonistic. None of that was conducive to physical training. Pushing the body without rest is counterproductive. But mentally... It separated the wheat from the chaff. And it prepared you for the what ifs.

What if your boat is hit and you find yourself on some foreign shore and there is no time to rest? Are you going to lie down and risk capture? Or being shot?

What if some adversary is yelling at you in a room with a light shining in your eyes, are you going to break and tell him everything?

Not only did your commander need to know the answers to these questions, but so did the sailor. Because, what if you find yourself in exactly this scenario?

INTO THE STORM

"Anderson!"

The soldier was racing past in a crouch as he yelled,

"GET OUT OF THAT MUD AND FALL BACK!"

The sound of bullets whistled past, mingling with the relentless drumming of rain on the muddy ground. Artillery explosions punctuated the air, sending shockwaves through the earth. Anderson was half buried in the mud, struggling to dig in. His company was retreating towards the tree line, leaving him scattered and exposed. His pack lay five feet away, his rifle was caked in mud, and he was up to his elbows in the muck, trying to free his small trench shovel.

"Why did I think digging in here was a good idea?" Anderson thought, his fingers numb from the cold and wet. The rain was relentless, each drop a tiny hammer against his helmet. He could taste the grit of mud in his mouth, feel it seeping through his uniform, chilling him to the bone.

"Join the army, they said. See the world," he grumbled.

He pulled the shovel free with a sucking sound just as a second soldier scurried by.

"Anderson! We gotta' move!"

Anderson quickly gathered his pack and rifle, falling to the ground to avoid the projectiles that seemed to be getting closer every second. He shoved the muddy shovel back into its loop and tried to pull the heavy pack over his arms. The weight of it pressed down on his shoulders, a familiar but unwelcome burden.

"Come on, move! You can't die here, not like this." The thought was a mantra, pushing him forward despite the fear gnawing at his insides.

Men kept racing past, their shouts barely audible over the rage of war that surrounded them. Now and then, another would yell for him to move. By now, he was dodging the bullets that smacked into the mud around him, trying to get his rifle, that he had foolishly laid down while wrestling the pack.

One lucky shot found the butt and ripped away a large fragment that tore through the air, finding the soft part of his cheek below his eye, tracing a bloody line across. The pain was sharp and immediate, a burning line of fire.

"Damn it!" Anderson rolled away from the rifle, deciding it was now a choice between dying and the trouble he would get into for not having that rifle. He crawled rapidly away from his muddy hole, back toward the trees where the last of his company was disappearing. Easing himself up into a crouch, he began to run.

The trees were right there, inches away. The smell of wet earth and rotting leaves filled his nostrils. And then a loud explosion percussed through his head, throwing him forward. A bright light blinded his vision, and he fell into the underbrush.

"Is this it? Is this how it ends?" The thought was fleeting as darkness closed in, the sounds of battle fading into a distant roar.

INTO THE JUNGLE

"Anderson!"

"Yeah!" Anderson shouted back, pulling the tangle of weeds from the jets of the PT boat. The humid air was thick with the scent of wet vegetation and the distant rumble of artillery.

"You take that piece of sh** back downriver to the camp!" The officer's voice was strained, barely audible over the cacophony of the jungle and the river.

Anderson glanced around. The other sailors were frantically engaged in a firefight, their attention fully occupied. The dense jungle on either side of the river seemed to close in, the sounds of insects and distant animal calls blending with the chaos of battle.

"Why me?" Anderson thought, but there was no time for hesitation. He climbed aboard the PT boat, the metal hull slick with rain and river water. The engine sputtered to life, and he felt a momentary relief as the boat began to move.

The river was a murky brown, its surface dotted with debris from the surrounding jungle. The oppressive heat made his uniform stick to his skin, and the air was filled with the smell of mud and decaying plant matter. He pushed the boat forward, his eyes scanning the banks for any sign of movement.

"Come on, move! You can't die here, not like this." The thought echoed in his mind as he navigated the treacherous waters. The jets of the PT boat roared, but he knew they could clog again at any moment, leaving him a sitting duck for enemy snipers.

Suddenly, gunfire erupted from the jungle. Bullets whizzed past, some striking the water with sharp splashes. Anderson ducked instinctively, his heart pounding in his chest. He pushed the throttle, urging the boat to go faster.

"Join the navy, they said. See the world," he grumbled.

The boat hit an underwater log, sending it briefly airborne. Anderson's stomach lurched as he fought to regain control. "Damn it!" he yelled, pulling back on the throttle. The boat landed with a jarring thud, but continued forward.

He pushed hard forward on the throttle and it stuck tight. Gunshots began to rake the side of the large boat. He wriggled, and ducked, still pushing and pulling until the lever broke free with a 'thunk' and the engines roared to life again.

A rocket-propelled grenade streaked from the jungle, hitting the side of the bow. The explosion was deafening, and the front of the boat disintegrated in a shower of metal and fire. Anderson was thrown backward, the force of the blast sending the remainder of the boat and him tumbling into the riverbank.

"Is this it? Is this how it ends?" The thought was fleeting as darkness closed in, the sounds of battle fading into a distant roar.

AWAKENING

Anderson's eyes fluttered open, the world around him a blur of shadows and muted sounds. He lay still, the pain in his side a dull throb. The ground beneath him was cold and damp, the smell of wet earth filling his nostrils. He could hear the patter of rain on the roof of the hut above. The rain was constant and relentless.

"Where am I?" The thought was sluggish, his mind struggling to piece together the fragments of his memory. He remembered the explosion, the blinding light, and then... nothing.

Above him, he could hear voices speaking in Korean. The words were unintelligible, but the tone was calm, almost soothing. He strained to listen, his heart pounding in his chest. "Are they friend or foe?" The question gnawed at him, but he was too weak to move, too disoriented to think clearly.

As he drifted in and out of consciousness, a memory surfaced. He saw his small son playing on the floor, his chubby hands grasping at a toy truck. His wife stood nearby, her eyes filled with worry as she watched him prepare to leave. He bent down, kissing her softly on the lips, then ruffled his son's hair. "I'll be back soon," he had promised, though he wasn't sure if he believed it himself.

The memory faded, replaced by the cold reality of his situation. The rain had soaked through his uniform, and he shivered uncontrollably. He could feel the mud caking his skin, the cold seeping into his bones. He closed his eyes again, the darkness a welcome relief. *"I have to survive. I have to get back." He grasped the thought, pulling him back from the brink of despair as his eyes closed again.

AWAKE

Anderson's eyes snapped open, the world around him a chaotic mix of shadows and noise. He lay half-submerged in the muddy riverbank, the wreckage of the PT boat looming above him. The air was thick with the smell of burning fuel and wet vegetation.

"What happened?" The thought was sharp, his mind racing to catch up with his surroundings. He remembered the rocket, the explosion, and then... darkness.

Above him, he could hear voices speaking in a language he didn't understand. The words were harsh, urgent, and he felt a surge of panic. "Are they coming for me?" The question sent a jolt of adrenaline through his body, but he was too weak to move, too dazed to think clearly.

He closed his eyes again, the darkness a brief respite from the chaos. "I have to survive. I have to get back." He clung to the thought that guided him through the fog of pain and fear.

"Anderson!"

The young man turned around, his eyes scanning the front of the recruiting station. The building was brick with large windows, posters of the Army, Navy, Air Force, and Marines displayed prominently. The air was thick with anticipation, the kind that comes with making life-changing decisions.

He took a deep breath, his heart pounding in his chest. The decision had been made, but the weight of it still pressed heavily on his shoulders. He glanced at the posters, each one depicting a different path, a different future.

"This is it. No turning back now." The thought was both exhilarating and terrifying. He squared his shoulders and stepped forward, ready to face whatever was on the other side of this door.

THE HUT

For Anderson, time passed in a haze of pain and confusion, each awakening marked by the murmur of voices above him. Sometimes they were close, other times distant, but always there, a reminder of his precarious situation.

Finally, he woke to a sharp pain in his chest. His breathing was distorted, a rattling noise emanating from his lungs. He fought not to scream out and managed to hold it in, perhaps because there wasn't enough air in his lungs to let it out.

He closed his eyes and lay there, listening. Everything was quiet. He held his position, making sure that his ears were still working. Nothing. No creaking floor, no voices, nothing dropping against the floorboards. Nobody home.

He tried to turn, and a small spattering of frothy blood seeped from his wound. He dropped back where he was laying and tried to catch his breath.

Slowly, he gathered himself and dug around in his pockets until he found what he was searching for: a white handkerchief. As gently as he could manage, he stuffed it into the hole in his side to slow the bleeding, biting a hole in his lip in the process.

Now he rested another moment and listened. Still nothing. Nobody home.

He closed his eyes and prepared his mind for the pain he knew was coming. Then he rolled over. This time he couldn't keep it in. A short and sharp "eahh!" escaped. He froze in his spot and listened. Nothing. Nobody home.

And he began to crawl. He felt the dampness and the sun on the side of his face. He couldn't be sure, but guessed morning. So, he put the sun on his left cheek and began to crawl toward what he hoped was south.

The journey was agonizingly slow. Each movement sent waves of pain through his body, but he pushed on, driven by the thought of survival. The landscape around him was a blur of mud and foliage, the rain-soaked ground making every inch a struggle. He could hear the distant sounds of battle constantly reminding him of the danger he was in.

Hours passed, or maybe days. Time had lost all meaning. His vision blurred, and he felt the world spinning around him. But he kept moving, inch by inch, through the tall grass and underbrush.

Finally, he saw a jeep beyond the grass and watched it approach. He could recognize the sound of those gears anyplace. IT WAS A JEEP. IT WAS THE ARMY!

He pushed through the weeds and into the road, waving one arm in the air as his legs gave out and he fell to his knees.

He couldn't remember if he passed out right there in the road, or in the arms of the soldiers as they put him in the jeep that day. The next time he woke up was in a field hospital. They had two or three bags of fluids piped into his arms and patches on his ribs with bandages wrapped around him. The beeping and whirring of medical equipment filled his ears like the sound of crickets at night back home.

It seemed like forever at the time, but then everything happened so fast. He was up and limping into a plane with a handful of papers in a manila envelope and a small bag with his few possessions.

As the plane left the runway, a warm feeling went through his whole body. All of the tension released at once. He was free. He was alive, and he was going home.

But then, as the trip went on, that feeling was replaced. The memories of the men that didn't make it off the field that day. They came in rushes. Vivid and full color. The images he wouldn't describe. And then the other men in his company. The ones he was leaving behind. The ones that were still alive.

He shook it off... For a while.

THE BOAT

Anderson's eyes snapped open, the world around him a muffled mix of shadows and noise. He lay half-submerged in the muddy riverbank, the wreckage of the PT boat wrapped around him like a coffin. The air was thick with the smell of fuel and wet vegetation. The oppressive heat made it hard to breathe, and he could feel the sweat mixing with the mud on his skin.

"What happened?" The thought was sharp, his mind racing to catch up with his surroundings. He remembered the rocket, the explosion, and then... darkness.

Above him, he could hear voices speaking in Vietnamese. The words were harsh, urgent, and his mind filled with panic. "Are they coming for me?" The question sent a jolt of adrenaline through his body, but he was too weak to move, too dazed to think clearly.

The rain was pouring, each drop was like a tiny hammer against the remnants of the boat. The jungle around him was alive with the sounds of insects, and distant gunfire surrounded him like a black cloud. He could feel the river water lapping at his legs, the mud sucking at his boots as he tried to move.

Time passed in a haze of pain and confusion. Anderson drifted in and out of consciousness, each awakening marked by the murmur of voices around the boat. Sometimes they were close, other times distant, but always there to remind him of his present situation.

Finally, he woke to a sharp pain in his leg. His breathing was distorted, a rattling noise emanating from his lungs. He fought not to scream out and managed to hold it in, maybe because there wasn't enough air in his lungs to let it out.

He closed his eyes and lay there, listening. Everything was quiet. He held his position, making sure that his ears were still working. Nothing. No footsteps, no voices, nothing dropping against the boat. Nobody home.

He tried to move, and a small spattering of blood seeped from his stained pant leg. He dropped back where he was laying and tried to push away the pain. Slowly, he gathered himself and dug around in his pockets until he found what he was searching for: his field knife. As gently as he could manage, he cut himself free.

Now he rested another moment and listened. Still nothing. Nobody home.

He closed his eyes and prepared his mind for the pain he knew was coming. Then he rolled over. This time he couldn't keep it in. A short and sharp "eahh!" escaped. He froze in his spot and listened. Nothing. Nobody home.

He began to dig with the knife, using the rainwater streaming under the boat to help make a small path to escape his confinement. He got out from under the boat and made a stumbling dash into the trees to hide.

The jungle was dense, the foliage pressing in on all sides. Now he could see how badly his leg was torn open. He sat down and dug through his pockets to find a white handkerchief. He tore open his dungarees and wrapped the wound as best he could, biting a hole through his lip in the process.

His escape from here was punctuated with the voices of Vietnamese soldiers in the jungle, but eventually, he found some solitude. A long stretch of quiet jungle. He continued on, each step a struggle, his vision blurring from the pain and exhaustion.

Suddenly, the sound of a pair of Jacuzzi jets commanded his attention. He turned and made a clumsy run in the direction of the river. Sliding off the edge of the bank, he nearly fell in. He waved one arm in the air, while holding onto some roots with the other.

The PT boat engine dropped its roar to a hum and turned in his direction. His mind must have reached its limit because everything else was just little glimpses in his memory. The men talking to him as they were lifting him out of the water. A face speaking at him with the sky behind it. The sound of the wheels on the gurney as they ground away on the concrete beneath them.

And then the weeks in the hospital. It seemed like forever. Why couldn't they just get it over with? Then it all happened at once. The wheelchair to the plane. Hands pulling and lifting, and he was in the air. All of the tension released at once. He was free. He was alive, and he was going home.

But he turned to look out the window, and below were his friends, waving from the ground. The ones he was leaving behind. The ones that were still alive.

He put it out of his mind... For a while.

AWAKENED

"Anderson!"

The young man turned around to see his dad and grandfather in the car. His dad was pulling his prosthetic leg out of the sill, then limping toward him.

His grandfather remained in the car, attached to the tube that fed fresh oxygen into his nostrils. The old man's eyes were sharp, despite the frailty of his body.

"I'm signing up, Dad. I made my decision." Young Anderson was firm in his plans, but he thought it must be important if Grandpa was in the car. It was an act of Congress and an all-hands-on-deck mission to get him out of the house.

"I know, son. We just need to talk first. There are some things you need to know." His father's voice was steady, but there was a weight to it, a gravity that made young Anderson pause.

He looked at his grandfather, who nodded slowly. "Your dad's right. There are things you need to understand before you make this choice."

Young Anderson felt a lump form in his throat. He had always admired his father and grandfather, their bravery and sacrifice. But seeing them now, the physical reminders of their service, he felt a pang of fear. "Is this my future?"

Titles By JJ Caler

The Carrigan Chronicles

Lia's Odyssey

Coffee and Dreams

The Adventures of Jasper and Blejack

A Perfect Place

"At a time like this... Here in this perfect place..."

By Arya Anakin

Copyright © 2024 Arya Anakin

All rights reserved.

A Perfect Place

A SHORT STORY BY ARYA ANAKIN

THE THIRD TIME

At a time like this, here in this perfect place, at this very moment, I will get to see you again...

I waited.

The cold of the previous snowstorm was slowly giving way as dawn seeped in for sunrise. The sun was already peeking through the horizons, tiny golden rays twinkling over the white flakes that spread on the concrete floor like a carpet. The air was still, the morning silent, or perhaps the town dwellers were yet to wake up, and even if some early birds were out already, sweeping the snow off the roads or salvaging household items left out accidentally through the night, it would still have been no distraction at all. The perfect place was far away from the town square, at the junction of the last roadside bench before the winding road spun wildly into a narrow route that led into the distant forest—forest now clad in flakes of snow.

I checked the time.

Just a few minutes before seven o'clock.

I heaved a sigh and realized just how dry my throat was becoming. My sinuses felt stuffed and my eyes blurry. The cold had hit hard, and it was going crazy on me. On a normal day, I would be locked up in my room, reading a book with a cup of coffee by my bedside.

Today wasn't a normal day, though. *He was coming.*

It was easy to become impatient—to begin to doubt if any of it was ever true. In another ten minutes, uncertainty began creeping in and I had to think that perhaps, just maybe, everything that had happened before had only been some programming of my mind. Was I too sad? Was I too lonely?

I checked the time again—for the sixteenth time since I had arrived, which was by half past six.

Seven o'clock.

I shook my head. *He's not coming, Jane. It's not real...* The whispers were now murmurs; the quiet talk was picking up volume. I rose from the chair and sighed, trying to blink in the tears that stung my eyes.

I'd be fine... I'd be fine... I took the first step forward.

"The winter came in rather quickly."

My breath hung in my throat as I turned to him, the mere sight of him filling me with adrenaline. Every bit of my existence instantly came to life as I ran for him and squeezed my arms around him. Now, the tears did fall and in quiet sobs, my arms wrung around him tighter, wishing to never let go.

Then I looked up at him, right into his hazel eyes. I had to make sure—I raised my hand and traced my fingers down his cheeks. He chuckled.

"Realer than ever." He whispered quietly. "Come here."

He pulled me close as I felt his tender lips enveloping mine and shut my eyes in ecstasy, feeling my fingers as they ran through his oily, brown hair. I wanted to enter him, to merge with him and become one forever and watch my loneliness vanish for good.

He broke the kiss now, just at the right time to catch my breath and then as he arranged my hair around my face, he smiled—the warmest smile life had ever blessed me with.

"You look beautiful today..." He whispered. "Left to me; I'll tell you that every day."

His words warmed my heart; I almost couldn't feel the snow anymore. "Well, you should see what I looked like last night... like an electrocuted dog."

"No..." He burst into laughter.

"I'm serious!" I continued. "My hair was all up, my nose runny, and my eyes swollen."

He laughed harder. "You, Jane... You never knew how to take a compliment."

I chuckled. "That's what I end up looking like on nights when you're not there."

He smiled warmly now as his gaze shifted away. I could see the topic was about to change. "How are you coping with the stress of your job?"

"Writing?" I laughed. "Writing was never stressful to me."

He made a face. "Okay, tell me you're not talking to your laptop."

"Alan!" I laughed.

"Or that you aren't yelling to a character like he'd ever listen."

"Stop!"

"Or that you aren't crying killing off one of your characters."

My mood suddenly shifted as he brought it all back to memory. "I'm writing a book about you, Alan." He stopped, staring right at me for a good while. I could see the tears in his eyes—not truly smiling nor truly crying. "Yeah, you..." It was hurtful; it was heart-aching to say the words. "You brought my writing back, Alan. You made the writer's block go away."

"Come here." He pulled me close as we settled back on the roadside bench. I leaned on his chest, feeling his heart beating within him. I knew his tears were on the brink of falling, and he didn't want me to see it, so this was his strategy—pull me close—too close so that I don't get to see the pain.

"So, how about you tell me about this story?" He whispered quietly, stroking my hair slowly.

"There's that one good, extremely intelligent graduate of Medicine who began an awkward career in music." He laughed in between and I chuckled. I continued, sniffing, holding back the tears. "...who met a delusional writer off the streets of California when they both got into an argument in a restaurant about the human chromosomes." He laughed again—the rhythm of his stroking fingers ever constant. "An argument would become the spark, birthing an unending love, one that could not be broken…" The words wouldn't come now. The emotions were welling up within me, and I felt the tear slipping down my cheek, and then resting on the coat he wore. His stroking had stopped, and I heard him sniff. He was crying. He was tearing up. I didn't need to look.

"When would you be back again?' I whispered quietly.

"At a time like this, here in this perfect place, in this very moment, I will get to see you again." He whispered back. "But here and now, draw close to me and never let go. *I am right here with you.*"

Then I was alone.

THE LAST TIME

3 weeks after the third time...

Day forty-three of coming to the perfect place.

It was still snowing. February was almost halfway in. The snow was lighter. My health was better.

I have come every day since the beginning. I managed to meet him only four times.

Today looked unlikely. From my observation during the last four times we had met, he came just before the sunrise and left when the rays were peeking out bright enough. At this point, the sun was already high enough. Morning had fully set in.

I checked the time.

8:00am.

In the earlier times, I had waited till nine in the morning before I observed that anything past eight meant he wasn't coming. It was okay to go back now. I had to feed Barry and take him to a vet afterwards. Then I had an appointment with my manuscript editor. One of my colleagues from college invited me to a house party tonight. I wasn't sure I would go but I could give it a try.

I think I was beginning to have schedules... *ever since I discovered this place.*

I sighed heavily as I stood. "Alright, let's go." I said to no one at all. I began to make my way back down the path I had come by when I heard the voice—his voice.

"Jane!"

I ran to him instantly and threw my arms around him. Every day the perfect place brought him to me, it felt different; like independent episodes, each offering a new experience that I always wanted to relive. He wrapped his arms around me tighter and then planted a kiss on my lips. It felt strange and new, feeling him.

"I just want to be here with you today. We don't have to talk about anything. Just let me hold you." He whispered to me as he enveloped me again in his warm embrace.

"Well, I want to pour out my entire life to you right now. It's all getting better, Alan."

"Really?" He gasped.

"Yes, with you here."

I caught a closer look at the expression on his face and was about to ask just before he spoke. "Jane..."

I tugged at his chin. "What is it?"

"Today is the crossing."

I wasn't sure what happened to me within those next few seconds. It was like I had blacked out just then and taken an escape from what my life would be without him.

Or maybe we could still talk something out.

"The crossing... does that mean... like, are you going to heaven... is heaven even real? What does that mean?" I knew the meaning. He did too but could not say a word. He was staring down, tears trapped in his eyelashes.

The crossing was going to take him away from me.

I held him like he was my oxygen and if he were the slightest distance from me, it would take my breath away. I tugged at his vest. "I can't live without you, Alan."

"Hey... hey... listen to me, Jane. That is a total lie."

"No."

"Yes, Jane. That is a lie you've been telling yourself, so you don't have to let go of me."

"Alan, stop."

"You feel guilty for nothing at all; you feel guilty for not being in that vehicle with me. You feel guilty for not being by my side. You feel guilty that if you move on, I'd never forgive you..."

"No."

"But hey..." He tilted his head to get my stare. "Do you love me, Jane?"

Tears ran like rivers down my cheeks. I couldn't control them. They wouldn't stop.

"Alan, please... you can't do this to me..."

"Do you love me, Jane?"

"Alan."

"Jane!'

"With everything that dwells within me—every step I take, every breath I draw in, every dawn, every sunset, every dream I live in. Everything in me wants you, Alan. I love you."

"Then... then, Jane. Jane, you have to promise me. You have to promise me you would live the life you're bound to live."

"Alan, please."

His voice grew shakier by the second. "Promise me, Jane. Promise me you would move on and find someone else and be happy and never come back to this place... that you would live the life of your dreams and become that which you've always dreamt to be."

"Alan!" I growled in a soul-writhing pain I could not explain. "Alan, you can't make me do this."

"Jane... if you don't, I would never forgive myself. I would regret ever coming to see you and then leaving you in that well of pain."

There was no other way. It was one of the two. I nodded now, unable to speak until he placed his index finger below my jaw and tilted my head upwards. *"I promise."*

He smiled, tears filling his eyes. I saw something, just then, something like I had never seen before. It was like his skin shimmered and glistened and in bits and fragments, it began to break away. In that split second, everything we'd been through together played like a tape in my head, like this was meant to be part of the process.

It brought me to remember how it began – *the first time.*

THE FIRST TIME

3 weeks before the third time...

I could feel autumn leaving, but I wasn't ready for winter. I had forced myself to get in the mood. It wasn't always like this. Winter was heavenly for me. It was a gift. When the snow came so heavy and everyone was locked in, I'd pick out my notebook from the shelf, click open a pen, sit at the edge of a window where I could look out and watch the snow bury the entire neighborhood in its immaculate white, and then I'd begin to pen down some of my most amazing ideas.

I had written my first best-selling book in the winter season.

I anticipated it.

This winter, though, was going to be different, and so would be Christmas, and New Year, and the next celebration that came, *and my entire life...*

I lay on my bed, my eyes staring up at the blank ceiling as I tried to hypnotize myself—stare into the nothingness until my mind went blank. I wanted to forget the mere fact that I was alive. I wanted to forget. I wanted all the pain to go away.

The hypnosis wasn't working, though. The radio beside me emitted the shrewd static voice of a reporter saying something about the snow heading east and predicted to fall in less than an hour. In the distance, I could hear Barry, the rottweiler he had bought two Christmases before, barking ceaselessly.

Both of these side noises were subconsciously plaguing my brain. I could feel it. Intensifying...

I slammed the radio quiet. That was one way to start. I sat up in bed now as I turned to the clock by my side.

6:35am.

It was still too early to have Barry barking out at God-knows-what. As for me, it was past my waking time. I was meant to continue my morning routine of jogging towards the far fields and back. The therapist had said it would help clear my head and keep my calories in check since

I had been sitting at home for months doing nothing at all.

Barry was still barking.

It was now beginning to play on my nerves. I shot up from the bed. *"Okay, buddy, thanks for waking me up since somehow, my alarm clock forgot to do its job, but that's enough!"*

The angry thought gave me strength I didn't know I had. I charged through the corridors of the cottage and lurched out onto the porch.

"Barry!'

The dog only stole a glance at me and instantly returned its eyes to whatever they were on before. The wind was picking up, and the trees were whistling wide, but the neighbors were all still in.

"Barry, what is going on?" I traced his stare but saw nothing... *at first.*

I looked at the dog again. Intense focus. I traced the stare back and shivered in shock.

"Alan!" I gasped in disbelief.

Then I remembered the therapist. *The drugs may have hallucinating effects.* My breath shuddered as I shut my eyes and shook my head in the same moment, my heart pounding in my chest.

Nothing.

Tears flooded my eyes as I reopened them. Barry whimpered beside me. *You'd seen him too?* Whining sadly, he strolled back into the house. It was happening again. I was seeing things again. I had to clear my head.

Instantly, I took off, running uncontrollably—not jogging, running non-stop. By the time I would be done, I would be too tired to think, and then it would be all gone—*all gone with the wind.* Tears streaked uncontrollably down my eyes as I thrust forward, running with the force of the wind, running through the streets as fast as my legs could carry me, wishing and longing for something—to die and let it all end.

I can't do it again, Alan. I can't do it again!

I ran.

I can't...

I never wanted to stop.

I can't live any more...

I crashed against a bench by the side of the road and broke down in loud sobs, clutching my aching stomach as I slid to the ground, wishing at that moment to have death come and let it all be over.

Then something came.

I felt an arm—or two arms—wrap around me from behind.

"Jane..." The familiar voice whispered quietly.

I sobbed quietly now as I held *his* arms, the familiarity of the voice echoing in the depths of my soul. *Take me with you, Alan. I can't bare this torture anymore.*

"It's okay, I'm right here."

I paused.

Whatever drugs the therapist had given me, they were playing on me so terribly, and I could tell it wasn't going to end well... because how was it that I could sit here on this bare concrete floor, holding onto his arms and hearing his voice from behind me?

"I'm sorry, Jane."

I froze, unable to move, unable to tilt my head backwards to see what was behind me, unable to breathe. I lowered my eyes to the hands around me again. They were still there. Blinking hard enough and shaking my head always did the trick so I did just that. Then I opened my eyes.

His arms were still around me.

"I am right here."

I threw his arms aside and spun immediately, gasping for breath in the wind. And to the greatest impossibility, there he stood, staring back at me with a look of worry on his face.

Had I gone mad? *No... no... no... this was bad.*

"What's going on?" I couldn't tell if I was asking him or asking myself to talk myself into reality again.

"You can see me, Jane?"

What?

I opened my mouth to speak but there were no words. "What is going on?"

His face eased into a smile slowly, one of hope and overwhelming joy. "It worked! I can feel you. You can feel me. *You can see me!* This is the perfect place!"

He moved to come closer but I drifted backwards. As good as this was, it could never be true. This was my mind, and I needed to get the hell out of it.

"Alan... I... You can't be here."

Alan smiled. "I know, but this is different. This is a perfect place! *At a time like this, in this very moment, anything you wish for will be yours, here in this perfect place.*" It was like he had quoted something. "It's something about the coincidences of our lives and this place. It fuses our worlds together."

Screw this!

Two steps and I had my arms around him as he burst into laughter with gratitude, garnished with tears flowing down his cheeks. I ran my fingers around his face. *The wounds... they were gone.* I kept feeling him—his hair, his eyes, his lips, his nose, his skin... It was difficult to get it done with.

"Alan, is this real?" I asked with my shaky breath, finding it more difficult than ever to speak. "Alan, is this happening? Are you back to me?"

There was a streak of concern on his face as he cupped my face in his arms. I stared into his eyes and was lost there for a good while. "I am yet to cross over, Jane." He replied softly. "So, while that wait happens, I would get to meet you in this very place at a time like this."

"Every day?"

He smiled. "It happens like striking a match. You may strike the surface over and over, but it doesn't pick the light until one spontaneous time; it just takes place."

"How did this happen? How did you know this would happen?" I gave him some space, trying to comprehend it all. I needed to understand. Perhaps if I understood what exactly was happening right now, then I could find a way to be with him for good.

"I don't know, Jane. I just knew it. I just found myself here at this right time. It was almost like you wanted me here so badly that it did bring me here."

Oh, if only he knew. "I want you everywhere I go so badly, Alan." I replied as I wrapped my arms around him. "Can I stay here with you forever?"

"I don't think I can remain around for much longer." He replied as he placed a kiss on my forehead. "But I think this can happen again."

"I would come here every day!" I stated clearly.

"And so will I."

"Please don't go without me. Don't leave me, Alan." I panicked.

"Hey... hey, listen." He held my face up to him. "I am always with you... I love you, Jane."

I shut my eyes as I kissed him again and again.

And then the wind blew.

And I was alone.

Now even as I stood before him, I remembered much beyond the memory of both of us. I remembered everything.

The meeting in the restaurant... the argument... the dates... the marriage... the dreams... the vehicle... Alan in his Cadillac, crushed within the two colliding trucks... his body reassembled from bits... the phone call.

"Can you identify this body?"

It was Alan Wilkerson. He was my husband.

And he was dead.

***

"You look beautiful today." He whispered. The glow was getting brighter. I shielded my eyes.

"Alan!" I screamed in agony, choking, calling again on death.

"In a perfect place, right there in your heart, I would be with you, Jane. I will always be with you."

I reached for him. Got a piece of his shirt. Wrapped my arms around his shoulders. Planted a kiss on him. Feeling the tears run down my eyes. Feeling the tears run down his eyes.

"Goodbye, Alan."

Light.

Bright light.

And, then I was alone.

Titles By Arya Anakin

Root of all Evil

By Daniel Nick

Copyright © 2024 Daniel Nick

All rights reserved.

DANIEL NICK

A Short Story by
Daniel Nick

THE ROOT OF ALL EVIL

DANIEL NICK

IN THE BLOOD

"It's in the blood my boy, it's in the blood." My boss smiled as he said that, as if he didn't know how shitty it made everyone but his own kid feel, especially my boy.

Hell, there was something to it though. After all, his kid was as big a shit as Morelli was. Show off. The kind of kid that would pull the wings off flies and...damn, the brat didn't even deserve the cliché.

Morelli had worked long and hard at this annual father and son get-togethers to provide his kid with plenty of opportunity to show off. And the damnable thing was that the little shit Finney was good. He was a hell of an athlete; ran like a fucking deer.

Phineas Morelli, son of Bartholomew Morelli. A bully raising his son to be worse than him.

"Good try Sammy," I called over to my son. He, as usual, had to try to guard against Finney during these flag football games. Poor Sammy was fourteen, the same age as Phineas, and Bart's rules were pretty clear about who had to guard whom. Age was the "fair" way to divide up the coverage assignments.

Never mind that despite the fact that Sammy was adopted, he was built just like me. We were born to be lineman, not a damn Gazelle. This was the fourth touchdown Finney had scored against my boy.

"Huddle!" called Bart. The bastard was going for two. Any guess who was going to get the ball?

"Come here, Sammy. Come over here guys," I called to the rest of our despondent team. Wearily, they formed a raged circle around me.

"Alright," I said, "We know what's coming. They're just going to try to get it to Finny again. Sammy, don't let him off the line. Stop him right there. He can't catch the ball if he's not in the end zone, right?"

"Sure thing, Dad." He looked less than sure.

"It's just a game son, none of this means a damn thing tomorrow." He looked at me with one of those faces that teens reserve for when adults say something particularly stupid, but at least he held his tongue.

The other team lined up on the ball and Bart got behind the center Mitch Greenwood, the corporate yes-man. I glanced over and saw the look of dismay on my son's face. In a fraction of a second I understood. Finny was lined up at least five yards behind the line of scrimmage. With the flag football rules that we had, Sammy wasn't allowed to cross the line until the quarterback threw the ball. By then it would be too late. Finney would have a five-yard cushion of space around him. Sammy didn't have a prayer.

I felt a righteous rage suffuse me. Sammy may have been beat, but I wasn't. As the man assigned to guard the quarterback, I was the only one allowed to rush across the line when the ball was snapped. Bart never worried about me because...well...he was the damn boss and I was his employee. Not this time. When the ball was snapped, I charged across that line like it was the final play of the super bowl. I don't know what the hell Bart saw in my face, but I saw abject terror on his--way out of proportion to the situation, but I didn't care, he wasn't getting that pass off to his kid.

When I hit him, I felt rather than heard the sickening crunch of Bart's ribs as I totaled him. He went down like a redwood under the axe.

I stood over him and snarled, "Didn't score on my boy this time, did you?"

"It was the blood that got me." I said as I set my coffee down on the table in front of me. "When I saw blood on his lips after that tackle, I thought that I had punctured his lungs or something. I didn't realize that it was just from his nose!"

The whole table broke up into laughter. Crushing my boss at the picnic was turning into the best career move I'd ever made. It had been three weeks since the incident, and nobody seemed to be getting tired of the story.

Of course, I should have been terrified of the repercussions. Everybody knew Bart didn't hesitate to fuck with people he didn't like. The company had his name on it, so he could do pretty much anything he wanted to do. In fact, he had - many times. That first day back to work was torture because I was sure that he was going to find some way to end my job. He loved to bully us all, and he had an almost pathological need to appear invincible and in charge.

Hell, he had fired Tommy Sharps just for taking the wrong side in a meeting with prospective clients. Ruined his whole career by charging him with theft. Pressed charges and everything, even though he knew Tommy hadn't stolen shit. He really did it just to show us who was in charge.

So why was I still here? In the three weeks since the "tackle that shook the world" as my coworkers called it, Bart had not only left me alone, he had outright avoided me completely. I saw fear in his face whenever he looked at me.

I couldn't figure it out at all.

Meanwhile, all the oppressed masses of Bartholomew Imports were crowding my table every day at lunch to hear the tale of the dragon slayer and his conquest. In fact, the only problem seemed to be my son. Every day when I came home to him and told him about my day he would ask the same two questions.

"Did you talk to your Boss today, Dad?"

"No Sammy, I didn't get the chance. We're all really busy at the office, Bart most of all, and we don't really get to see him whenever we want to. He kind of calls us when he wants to see us."

He didn't ever believe me of course, and his second question always proved it. "Did you talk about the game with anybody else?"

"Just a few of the guys at lunch, that's all."

He always looked at me with some indefinable emotion in his eyes, somewhere between pity and pain. I didn't understand why. It's been just he and I against this world since his mother passed away three years ago and we've grown to share a pretty special trust. That's why I just couldn't figure this funk he was in.

I asked him, "Finny hasn't been messing with you at school, has he?"

He lowered his eyes, as he answered, "No."

"Sammy, what's wrong?"

"Nothing."

"I don't think so, kid. What's the Real Deal?" I asked. The "Real Deal" was a slang term we had started using with each other years ago. It meant no lies, no evasions, and a promise of no judgment or repercussions. Anything said while in the "Real Deal" was protected.

He looked up and said, "Finny's not bothering me, Dad. In fact, he's spending all his time trying to be my friend. He..."

"What is it?" I prompted.

"Nothing."

"Sammy, you're starting to sound like a broken record. Now tell me what's going on."

He spit out all at once and all together, "Finny told me that his dad said to be my friend and treat me nice, and I don't like this. Not one bit. They're scared because you lost control. It's not right, Dad, and it shouldn't happen this way. They're not supposed to be frightened of us."

He jumped up from the table and ran upstairs to his room, too close to adulthood to cry, too young to stop the tears.

I sat there stunned. I didn't understand, at first.

That next day I stormed into Bosses office, blood boiling, yelling, "You got something going on involving my son. What the hell is it?" It was a beautifully dramatic moment and would have scared the shit out of Bart—if he had been there.

Feeling stupid, I went back to his startled secretary outside the office and asked her, "Where's the Boss?" She just stared at me blankly.

Taking a deep breath, I started again. "Hi Gladys. I'm an idiot, and rude too. Will you accept my apology?"

She smiled, "I guess the fact that you just yelled at an empty room is punishment enough, especially after I tell all the girls at lunch."

I had to laugh at myself, and felt a few knots of frustration and anger start to loosen. "Fair enough. So where is he?"

"Bart is taking the day off to be with his family."

"No, seriously Gladys, where is he?"

"I'm dead serious. He's with his wife and kid."

"But..."

"I know! It's the weirdest thing. He just called me about half an hour ago to tell me. You must have rattled his brains when you tried to kill him."

"Gladys." I warned. "Don't tease about that stuff. As a matter of fact, that's what I'm here about. Something's going on, or at least I think it is. I've got a feeling the bastard is up to something involving my son."

"Like what?" she asked with equal parts concern and avarice. I could see the gleam in her eyes as she asked. This could be good gossip.

"I don't know exactly. Revenge for the other week was my first thought, but now..."

"Now what?"

"Well, it just doesn't feel right. To be honest, I don't think of Bart as devious, just mean. Why would he go through the trouble? He could just pull a Tommy on me and I'd be gone."

"I know what you mean. Bart isn't smart enough to pull off a real slick revenge thing. Plus, it just isn't his style."

"Actually Gladys, this whole thing doesn't make sense. I mean, until today I wouldn't have thought that he would take the day off like this, either. I don't know what to think any more. This is a whole new Bartholomew Morelli."

"Yeah," she agreed, "and we might have you to thank for it."

"Don't thank me yet." I said, thinking of my last conversation with Sammy.

The following day I arrived at work to find a large crowd gathered around Mitch Greenwood. I couldn't hear what he was saying, but by the expression on his face, it was clear that he was out for blood.

They were all hanging out at the smoking area in front of the building, but I recognized several non-smokers. The quiet murmurings dwindled away to nothing as I approached.

"What's up fellas?" I asked.

Silence.

I looked from face to face. I didn't like what I saw. "Guys? Someone die?"

Joe from accounting cleared his throat and said, "Mitch is telling us some fairy tales..."

"Horror stories are more like it." interrupted Mitch's good friend, Daryl.

"He's been telling us about that game you guys played," finished Joe.

"Look guys," I said, "don't make this into a big deal. It was an accident, Okay? For Christ's sake, we were playing a rough game and things just got a little out of hand."

"This isn't about the game, it's about you." said Daryl.

"What about me?"

"Look," said Mitch, "I was there alright? I saw what happened; saw you too. You didn't..."

"Didn't what?"

He looked around nervously as if gathering strength from the others before going on. Finally, he said, "You didn't look ...normal. Your face was, well, not really human."

"What the hell are you talking about?" I asked, perplexed.

"I know it sounds weird, but I swear to god that you looked like a ...a...demon or something!"

"Mitch, this is not funny," I said. "You stop talking this shit right now."

"Or what?" he challenged, "Are you going to hurt me too?"

I was about to write him off as a loon, but then I saw the looks going around the circle. These guys believed him! They were all scared of me.

Stunned, I turned around and walked back to my car. For the first time in my entire career, I skipped work.

***

"Bloody hell!" my son said as his soda dropped to the floor. He bent over to clean it up, asking, "Did you talk to your Boss today, Dad?"

"No, Sammy, I didn't go to work.

He stopped halfway to his knees, rag in hand, "What?" he asked incredulously.

"I didn't go to work today."

"Are you feeling alright?"

I looked at him levelly, "I don't know, son." Then I proceeded to tell him about yesterday.

When I finished my story, Sammy sat for a few moments before he said, "Dad, some things can only be explained through family."

I was scared. My father used to say the same thing to me when I was a kid. It wouldn't have surprised me to hear it from my son if he had ever met my dad, but as my father had been gone for seven years before Sammy was even born, my surprise was total. I also knew that I had never said those words to him before, because I wasn't the least bit interested in being like my deadbeat father.

"Where did you hear that phrase?"

"Dad, you need to listen now, and don't freak out, O.K.?"

I nodded.

He took a deep breath, as if he was a father about to deliver the "Birds and Bees" speech. "Gramps. I heard it from Gramps. Do you understand what I'm saying?"

Impossible, and I said so.

"No Dad. It's possible, and I need you to believe me because what I've got to tell you now is way crazier."

"You're trying to tell me that my dead father has been talking to you, and that's not the crazy part?"

"Gramps never died, Dad. He just left you."

He was right of course, but I'd never told him that. Our official story was that Gramps had died before he was born, because we didn't want to explain to a toddler why Gramps would just walk out of the house one night and never return.

All I could think to say however, was "Just left us?"

"Dad..."

"Just left us doesn't do it justice son. The son of a bitch spent my whole life telling me about the bonds of family, and one night he just took off and never came back!" I was yelling at my son for the first time in his life, but despite my shame, I couldn't stop. "He was nothing but a lie, and if he's been sneaking around poisoning your mind with his twisted crap, then I swear to god I'll kill him!"

Sammy said to me quietly, "Revenge and punishment aren't our job, Dad. That belongs to different families." He glanced upwards as he said this as if looking for someone in the heavens.

"Son, what has that old liar been telling you?"

"Well, Gramps says our job is to...well...demonstrate the consequences of choices."

"What?"

"It's hard to explain."

"Well, why don't you try real hard?" I said sarcastically.

"I'm making a mess of this. I'm going to call Gramps and tell him to come over."

I was suddenly frozen. "You have his phone number?"

"Of course."

"You have my father's phone number. You talk on the phone to the man who walked out and abandoned his entire family over twenty years ago? That guy?"

"He had a reason, Pop. I know you hate him, but maybe it's time you two sat down and worked it out. He'll do this better than I can."

I stared at my son for a full minute before saying, "Yeah. Call the son of a bitch. I'd like to talk to him."

So, twenty-one years, five months, and three days after the man whose blood ran in my veins "went out for a beer", he came back and sat down in my living room.

He was uncomfortable and ashamed, I'll give him that much. He walked in the house looking at my son, around the room, and pretty much everywhere but at me. Finally, he took a seat and forced himself to look me in the eyes saying in that gruff voice I remembered from my childhood, "Hello son. I know you hate me, and I know you have every right to. I'd say I'm sorry, but that would probably just piss you off." He grimaced and shook his head. "Damn it. Still, for what it's worth, I am sorry."

I couldn't say anything that wouldn't have been a cliché, so I just held my tongue and crossed my arms, staring at him.

The silence stretched out too long and the whole room grew uncomfortable.

Finally, my son blurted out, "Just tell him, Gramps."

Still grimacing, he answered my son, "He won't believe me yet, Sammy. It's not something I ever shared with him."

"Shared what?" I asked.

"Who we are. What we are."

"What the hell are you talking about?"

"Son..."

"No," I interrupted, "No. You don't get to call me son. You spent years telling me all about how important family was, how strong our bonds were, and then you bailed. You're a liar. You are not my father, and I'm not your son. You call me Andy."

Sammy was agitated, "Dad, please stop and listen. Gramps can prove what he says, but it's...crazy. Well, that's what I thought at first. I thought he was a crazy guy living in some sort of delusion. But it's all true."

"What the hell are you talking about, Sammy?"

"I'm making a mess of this," he said while looking over to my father, "Please explain it, Gramps. He deserves to know."

My dad sighed again and looked at me, "I left you because you never came into your birthright. I had to leave because it would have been cruel and dangerous to stay. You would have been vulnerable and helpless."

Totally perplexed, I said, "What?"

"We are a special family, Andy."

"So, you said a million times when I was growing up."

"Well, we are. We are one of a few special lines that exist in this world. There are nine lines, to be exact, and we have a job."

"I don't understand anything you are saying."

"Dad, think of it like the seven deadly sins or something. Only there are nine. Nine transgressions against humanity, right Gramps?"

"Yes, Sammy. There are nine things that humans do to others that require...consequences. Nine family lines charged with delivering those consequences."

I turned to my son, "You said Revenge and Punishment are not our jobs. Is that what you meant?"

"Yeah, Dad."

"Son, you mean to tell me you believe this horseshit? Real Deal?"

"I've seen it, Dad. I...I came into the family charge two years ago."

"What the hell are you talking about?" I cried.

Then my father and my son turned into something inhuman right in front of me.

I may have fainted because my next memory is of sitting in a chair with a bloody lip as my father and son stood over me looking entirely normal.

"Sometimes it skips generations, son. I thought it skipped you. It did skip you."

I asked, despite knowing the answer, "What did?"

"Your family charge. You never changed. You stayed human your whole life. Until last week at least. That's a new one. Nobody has ever changed as an adult before. That boss of yours must be one serious bully."

Bemused yet still lost, I said, "The worst I've ever seen."

"He'd have to be. See, that's our job."

"What is?"

My son answered, "We show bullies the consequences of their actions."

"By tackling him and hurting him? That's ridiculous."

"No Dad, when you tackled him, you gave him a taste."

"A what?"

My father picked up the explanation and continued, "When we intervene in a bully's life, we give him a taste of what he's doing to others. Think of it kind of like that Christmas story by Dickens, they get visited by ghosts of bullying past, present, and future."

"They do?"

"No, of course not, but it's a nice visual. What they experience is the receiving end of all the bullying they've ever done or will do in their entire lives. One huge, violent, miserable snapshot of...them. Bullying themselves."

I was lost, scared, and angry. None of this made any sense. "How the hell do we do this crazy magic, huh? Let me guess; we wave our hands and say 'Boo!', right?"

"No, Dad. We...change...and we touch them. That's all it takes. Afterwards, we either work with them as an ally to help them change and grow, or we just leave. We have the choice to help them further or, if they have done one of the unforgivable sins, walk away. Those that haven't gone too far down the path of evil have the choice to change or continue their ways. If they continue, then they meet the...other... family. The one that punishes." he shuddered.

Gramps chimed in, "We don't help those that have crossed the line into true evil. We give them the glimpse, which usually shatters them mentally, and then we get out fast as Wrath will be on its way, and we can't be anywhere near it when it arrives."

"Okay. So, wait a minute here. You're telling me that nine families with magic blood run around the world righting wrongs and making people act nice? Some sort of magical superheroes working together to make the world a better place?"

"Oh no," Gramps answered, "Blood has nothing to do with it, obviously, " he said looking at my adopted son. "And the families don't get along at all. You are in mortal danger right now, son."

I was so confused I didn't even object to him calling me son again, "This is crazy. You have got to explain this to me better."

Sammy said, "There are nine family lines charged with guiding or correcting humanity dad, but we aren't all the same. There are three other families that we are 'related' to. The remaining five are...well...they're on the 'other side', so to speak."

"So to speak?"

"Yes."

"You're still not making sense."

My father got angry, "Yes, we are, son! You just don't want to listen. There are two sides out there, we are on the side of redemption and change. We give second chances if they deserve them, and we mark them for punishment if they don't. The other side gives punishment. Always. There is Good and Evil, son, and our family line was touched by good a long damn time ago. We are tasked with eradicating the root of all evil."

"Bullying?"

"Yes. If you take your time and really think about it, it's obvious. Imposing your will upon another simply because you want to and are strong enough to do it causes almost all of the world's ills. Not greed, not selfishness, not laziness.

Bullying. Making people do what you want, not through moral or ethical rightness, but simply because you are stronger. That's evil. It's Emotional abuse. Physical abuse. Rape. All of it is bullying at its core. The exercise of power because nobody can stop you. Well, we stop them if we can."

"We do?"

Sammy said, "We actually try to get them to stop themselves. Our weapons include fear, yes, but it's also empathy, sympathy, and emotional intelligence. That fear should be tied to enlightened self-interest."

"We try to fix rapists? Predatory pedophiles? What kind of sick joke is that?"

My son got serious and a little angry with me. "No, Dad, we do not. Evil people like that: we just mark them. They are beyond forgiveness once they make those choices. There is no redemption for evil that deep. Predators meet Wrath. Always.

"For others, though? People like your boss? We are supposed to make people better, Dad, not terrify them into running away. And we never use it for personal gain," he said, staring at me, willing me to get it.

I got it. "Like making my job easier and scaring my boss into being afraid of me?"

"Yeah Dad, you're at risk of turning into a bully yourself. If you do? Every other family will tear you apart. Literally."

I looked from my father to my son and realized they were absolutely serious, and they were scared. "What can I do? Is this really real?"

"Yes son, it's very real."

"Yeah Dad, it is."

"Well, what should I do?"

My father answered, "You've got to fix it. Fast. You need to talk to your boss. Make it right. Then we have to move."

"Move?"

"Yes, son. Move. That's why I left you. I had worked in the area we had lived in for a long time, and the other families knew about me, could find me. That's the life we lead. As agents of redemption, we are targets of the five families of punishment. They do not like us taking away their victims. At all. They'd kill us if they could. They do kill us if we're not careful."

He sighed and rubbed his eyes, "Your mother was tired of moving all the time and wanted out. We had drifted apart over the years and I knew she was about to ask for a divorce. You? You never came into your charge, so there was no way you were going to be able to protect yourself from our enemies. So, I let you both go. I left, taking the danger with me."

"So how did you come to start talking with my son behind my back?"

"Well, I left, but I didn't just turn my back forever. I loved you, son." He saw the anger come back to my face, flushing it red, "I know, that makes it worse in some ways, but it's true. So, I watched from a distance. I kept tabs on you and your mom, then when you had a son, I made sure to keep an eye on him in case the family charge picked him."

I held up a hand, "This is where you lose me. How can Sammy be part of this? Dora and I couldn't have kids, so we adopted Sammy." I repeated, "How can he be part of this?"

My father frowned as if I had disappointed him, "Are you really asking that, son?"

"Yes!"

"Is Sammy your son?"

"Of course," I said at once.

"In every way?"

"Yes."

"So, what are you confused about? This charge runs in families, not something as mundane as blood or genetics."

It was at that point that I finally believed them both. It's the only option when you hear the Truth.

***

We almost pulled it off without any bloodshed.

Almost.

We worked out a plan, and when my boss got back in town, I went straight to his office to see him.

He was not pleased to see me. He was still scared, but now I knew why.

"Bart?"

Looking up at me, his eyes clouded and his hands began to shake just the tiniest bit. "Yeah?"

"Can I take you to lunch? I need to apologize to you and explain a few things."

"You want to take me to lunch?"

"Yeah. And apologize."

"To me?"

"Yeah."

He seemed to think about it for a minute and then he shook his head, "Nah, it's fine. We're fine. No need to apologize for anything."

I walked over to his desk and sat down in the chair facing him, "Yes there is, Bart. This is serious. Please let me do this.

I won't force you to, or demand it, but I am asking sincerely."

He stared at my chest for almost a full minute before he worked up the courage to meet my eyes and say, "Alright."

I took my victory and walked out, thanking him. Then I went straight to Mitch Greenwood and his group of sycophants hanging around the water cooler and told them, "Bart and I are going to lunch today, Mitch. Hold down the fort while we're gone? Maybe stake a vampire or kill a werewolf while you're at it?"

Nobody laughed, but I turned on my heel and left immediately afterward because the point of that was to make his stories about me seem a little ridiculous. It didn't matter if they laughed or not, but it did matter that they stop listening to his stories about my transformation into a beast as if it was true. In time it would fade away as long as I could help Bart heal and change.

We went to lunch and I followed my long-lost father's advice and treated Bart as if we were old friends, speaking frankly and sincerely about my apologies for the way I had behaved at work after the "event".

He was surprised, "Oh. I thought you were going to apologize for...you know...hitting me so hard?"

I sat still and relaxed my body while saying, "Definitely not. That experience is called a 'taste', Bart. That was on purpose. You know what it was, right?'

Tears sprang to his eyes and he looked down at the tablecloth in shame.

Calmly, I said, "Bart? You need to answer me. It's important that you do."

Eventually he whispered, "Yes. I know what that was. It was me."

"It's what you are behaving as, not what you have to be. Change is possible Bart."

"No, Andy. That was me, my...evil. It was my past, my present, and my future." He started crying openly, "I could tell. I could feel it. I knew it as sure as I'm sitting here talking to you."

"Bart, look at me." I'll give him credit. He forced his head up to look at the monster that had destroyed his entire worldview. "I'm telling you that you can change. Me. If you trust anything about this crazy situation, trust this. I know what I'm saying, and it's the truth. You have a deep well of good in you." And as I said it, I realized it was true. I could tell with absolute certainty that Bartholomew Morelli had survived a childhood of bullying and learned to imitate his oppressors, but he didn't want to. He just didn't know how to break the cycle.

"Are you sure?" he asked.

"Absolutely, my friend. Let me show you how."

He smiled at me then. A genuine smile, and I thought that we might just make all of this work out after all.

As I left lunch and went to my car, I called my father and Sammy to tell them the good news. We were all feeling really good about the result of the talk.

But he was waiting for us at the office.

"It used to be like squeezing blood from a stone to get him to approve time off, but this morning..." Gladys trailed off from her gossip with Mitch as Bart and I walked off the elevator after returning from lunch.

Bart smiled at them both and said, "Hello you two. How are things going today?"

Gladys smiled and said, "Everything is fine, Mr. Morelli."

"Actually," Mitch said, "can I speak to you both in your office, Mr. Morelli?" Then he turned to Gladys, saying, "Could you be a dear and go grab us some coffee?"

Astonishingly, Gladys just smiled and left to get them.

I turned to Bart to see him just as surprised as I was, and then turned back to Mitch to say, "How did you do that? Gladys would have torn my head off if I asked her to go get me a coffee."

Unsmiling now, Mitch just said, "Gladys and I understand each other. Let's talk. Now."

Uneasy, I went into Bart's office behind the two men. Mitch went through first and was standing at the door and ushered me past him as he closed it.

Bart went to his desk, sitting down and asking, "What can I do for you, Mitch?"

With a deep, raspy voice coming from a throat not at all human, he answered from behind me, "You can accept your punishment after I'm done with him."

And talons stronger than steel wrapped around my throat and began to squeeze.

Bart began screaming a high pitched, almost falsetto squeal of terror as I tried to spin around to face my enemy. I immediately understood it to be one of the other families concerned with punishment. Mitch was one of the adversaries. It figured.

But he was in his altered form and he had me dead to rights, so it was a race to see if he would choke me out or break my neck first. As his claws drew little trails of blood from my skin and my vision began to fade out, I heard a crashing, tearing sound as if a battering ram was smashing through a castle wall and then it all went dark.

My last thought was for my son. He was about to lose his father and it broke my heart.

For a second time, I woke up with my father and my son dabbing at blood on my body.

Disoriented, I crazily thought that I might still be in our living room and that everything that had happened after I had fainted at the sight of them transformed had been a dream.

But no. This time I was on the floor of Bart's office, and Bart was right there with my family, helping to tend to my wounds.

I managed to rasp out, "What happened?"

Sammy smiled and said, "I'm sorry Dad, but the house is a wreck."

"What?"

My father said, "The Wrath family found us. Turns out 'ole Mitch there is the patriarch of the group and sent his son to kill Sammy while he planned to deal with you. I guess they didn't know I was around...heh, heh."

Still stunned, I could only repeat, "So what happened?"

Sammy stopped smiling, "We had to kill him. Gramps killed him. I...saw it. Then we realized what it meant and we hauled our butts over here as fast as we could."

My father said, "We ran into that gal Gladys. She saw Sammy as we came in and called out that she was getting coffee for you all. So, we crashed the party. Sammy saved your life."

I looked over at Sammy and he was looking down in embarrassed pride. "You did?"

He mumbled, "Sort of."

"Sort of my butt! I smashed the door down and Sammy crashed straight into his back, jumping on and putting him in a choke hold. He let go of you to deal with Sammy and then I got there. It was over pretty quick after that.

"Mitch is dead?"

"Oh no. He's right there," he said, pointing to the corner of the office.

Mitch was sitting in the corner, trussed up with zip ties – where the hell had they got zip ties from? – and crying.

I sat up slowly as Bart took over the story. "Your family subdued Mitch and your dad zip tied him up when he... changed back. Then your son apologized to him and told him his son had died. He's been crying ever since."

I turned to my son, "You apologized? For what?"

He turned to me with a serious expression on his face, "We don't do punishment, Dad. We do Redemption. His son's death was an accident."

"But they tried to kill us!"

My father stood up and put his hand on my son's shoulder, "We. Don't. Do. Punishment. Self-defense is one thing, but never on purpose, Andy."

I looked over at Mitch. He was still crying, but his eyes pinned mine with a loathing bordering on supernatural. I didn't care, the feeling was mutual. I stood up all wobbly but made my way over to him before kneeling down again. "Bart is on the path of redemption now. He is not yours. You will leave and never come back."

He sneered through his tears, "I know my charge, you weak little shit."

"Good," I cut him off, "Then go get your boy's body from our house and go away. I'm sorry for your loss."

My father cut him free without comment and Mitch left in silence.

Eventually, Bart asked, "Was Mitch always here to kill me?"

"Maybe," my father replied, "but maybe he was here hoping to get both you and my family. Either way," he continued, "you are safe from him now so long as you make a sincere and honest change."

"How can you be sure?"

"There are checks and balances for all of the families."

Bart gulped audibly, "All of the...you mean there are more of you?"

Briefly, I was tempted to tease Bart, but I had made strong inroads today with him and he needed kindness right now, not jokes and sarcasm. "Yes, Bart, but you will never meet them. I'm here to help you with that. As long as you need me."

"You really mean that, don't you?"

"Yes, I do."

"Why? I mean, thank you and all, but why? We're not even blood."

I looked at my son, then my father, and finally back to Bart. "Blood is irrelevant, Bart. Blood is nothing but a mundane bodily fluid. It has no special, mystical property. Family is special. It can be a choice. I'm giving you the opportunity to choose to earn your way into mine. To make yours worth being a part of for others. That's how you'll break this cycle of abuse and bullying."

He just stared at me.

Finally, I asked the only question that mattered, "Are you in?"

He stood up and shook my hand.

Titles By Daniel Nick

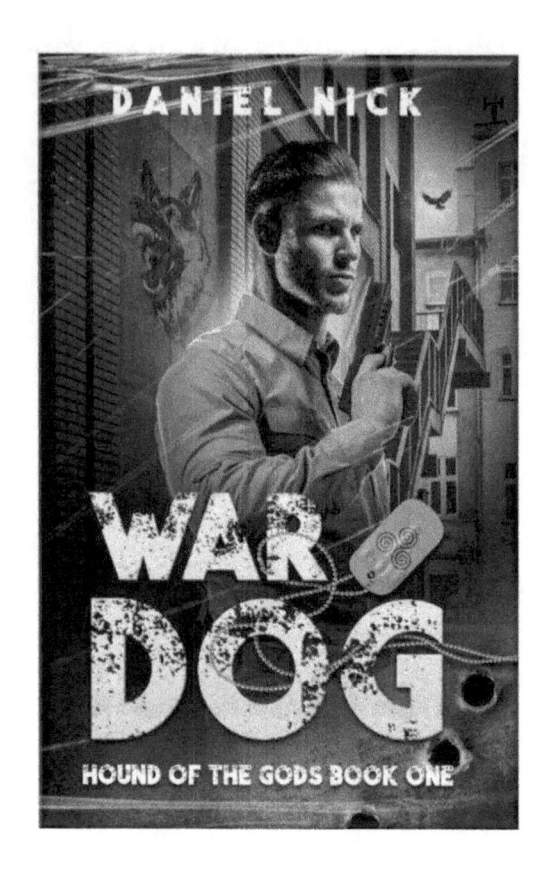

Chit Chat

By J Lee Bagan

Copyright © 2024 J Lee Bagan

All rights reserved.

A Short Story by
J LEE BAGAN

NEDHA'S
BEAUTY PARLOUR

CHIT
CHAT

NEDHA

The shop was small, somewhat, but not aggressively tacky, and a permanent fixture on Sub-Level 3. It had just enough room to fit two workstations along the left wall, along with one ancient bee-hived shaped hair dryer. A magazine littered demi-sofa and end table sat on the opposite side. The narrow ledged counter just inside and facing the front door completed the furnishings. The sign in the faux window, though as old as the shop itself presented a sharp contrast with its loud cheerful letters. Its bright pink neon proudly proclaimed to all that this was NEDHA'S BEAUTY PARLOUR. However humble its appearance, sooner or later, every woman on Reagan 4 came to Nedha's salon.

Inside Nedha's salon, the pseudo coffee was always hot, the magazines were at least of the current year, and conversation kept the constant loneliness of deep space at bay. If you were really lucky, your hairdo came out acceptable. But mostly they came to talk, to gossip, to act like women.

Reagan 4 was a mining base and not a very large one at that. A working crew of less than one-hundred men sufficed to extract the valuable Cesium from the ore pockets of Pollucite. On Garfield 9 they were mining the even rarer Platiniridium with a crew alone of fifteen-hundred.

The company allowed married men who worked the mines to bring their wives with them as long as they had no children or dependents, and if their contract was in excess of five years. If a woman became pregnant while on the asteroid, she was immediately returned to her home planet or moon. It was a standard non-negotiable clause found in every miner's contract throughout the belt.

The absence of children coupled with the bizarre subterranean lifestyle, of itself, was enough to quickly drive many a woman back to the familiarity of her homeland. "Thank you very much, but they didn't love any man enough to live like this."

The ones who stayed made all the necessary adjustments. They learned the proper way to suit-up for going topside, learned to prepare and eat foods they hadn't known existed even a short while back. Most of all, they learned to keep a tight rein on their emotions. Their men loved them dearly.

Nedha loved the ladies too, though some more than others. They gave her life warmth and purpose. She was a company widow, allowed to remain only because she had such a 'nice little business' going. Also, a particular company advisor had enough sense to know that the beauty shop was a vital emotional crutch for the womenfolk. It gave them a place to congregate in twos and threes, to let their hair down in more ways than one. A place with 'atmosphere'. Sort of like the MINER'S PUB on Sub-Level 2. (Women were not allowed on Sub-Level 2). Mr. company advisor never bothered to mention at the company meetings that he knew about this line of reasoning because his wife had coached him. Neither did he like sleeping alone.

No one knew much about Nedha's past. She was a Geyserian. The funny little ears and wrinkled nose gave that away. But otherwise, she blended well with the general female population. How she had come to meet and marry an earthman remained somewhat a mystery. Alas, true love has no boundaries and it was suspected her interracial (in the true sense) marriage crossed a culture barrier her family could not and would not tolerate. The Geyseri were by nature a socially private species to an extreme degree. They maintained inter-space contact only so far as necessary to conduct business and trade. Tourism was not encouraged and rarely allowed though not completely unheard of. Nedha volunteered nothing and only an occasional, ignorant newcomer tried to ask personal questions of her.

Without exception, the current ladies of Reagan 4 adored Nedha. She listened to their problems, laughed at their jokes, and did strange new things with their hair. She provided a place to chatter and ease their boredom. It didn't seem to matter to her the jokes and problems were pretty much interchangeable from patron to patron. Altogether, a rather placid existence.

That is, until the arrival of Mrs. Gina Fenley.

Gina Fenley admitted to being forty years old, forty-five would have been more accurate. She was, indeed, quite attractive, a face and figure based on good genes instead of good surgery. Her natural personality was animated and bubbly. It seemed as though she never stopped talking. You didn't have to like her, but you had to like her style.

Gina unabashedly like men. Adored them without pretense. The fact that she had never figured out how to get along with them did nothing to dampen her fondness for them. Four marriages and three divorces (rumor had the fourth well on its way) had eventually brought her to Reagan 4. Husband Roger was a deep-core engineer but Gina didn't care about that. She cared that he was ruggedly handsome, flirtatiously charming, and generous with his physical affections.

Twice a week now, Mrs. Gina Fenley breezed into Nedha's modest little shop spreading gaiety and good-natured complaints about men in general. Nedha genuinely liked her and looked forward to her visits. Today was Thursday, and Gina had a Two-o'clock appointment.

In she blew, but ten minutes late. "Oh! Nedha honey, I know I'm late but the tram was crowded and Roger and I had a fight; over something silly, I suppose. It always is, you know. Oh my, it just hasn't been my day at all, dear. Listen honey, can you do me up real nice. We're supposed to have dinner with the Ballards and..."

Gina Finley had arrived.

Gina chattered like a squirrel right on through the shampoo and trim, going on about the shortage of pantyhose, dull movies at the rec-hall cinema, and what a rotten dancer Roger had turned out to be.

CHIT CHAT

"Honey, at Suz and Jim's anniversary party last week, that man stepped on my toes so much I had bruises on them. No fooling, I did. He might be a hunk and all but he's a clumsy one." Nedha nodded in all the appropriate places, took a quick break to refresh Gina's coffee, then continued snipping and shaping the marvelously long and golden tresses in her care.

Gina never missed a beat. "Anyway, honey, he got all mad and huffy because I danced a tune or two with Dennis Owens, you know him, don't you? Now there's a hunk who can certainly dance a smooth one. Single too. You ought to give old Dennis the eye, honey. He'd be a sweet catch for someone—ouch! Think you missed a tangle or two, honey. Be careful."

Nedha couldn't help it, she laughed right out loud. Mrs. Fenley sure livened up the place. "So, you need to look special tonight. Did you have some particular style in mind?"

"Listen, honey, you know them plastic plunger looking thingies you put up on top and then wrap the curls around? Well, is mine long enough for that?" Nedha nodded. It was. Gina stopped talking just long enough to sip at the fresh cup of what passed for coffee.

"Listen, Nedha honey. I know folks are whispering about me and Roger. Not that it bothers me too much. I know scenes like at the rec-hall last night get around fast. But I want you to know now, I don't hold nothing personal against Roger, really, I don't. He's a way nice fella, he is, and I do love him...." She sighed, deeply, no doubt for effect. "We just don't seem to get along so well anymore. You know what I mean? I guess maybe it really is mostly my fault. But, as much as I like men, it just never seems to work out. It's not fair, you know."

Though Nedha wasn't liking this sadder side of Mrs. Fenley, she had to ask. "What isn't fair, dear? What do you mean?"

"Why honey, men are the only opposite sex we have to choose from. I mean, it ain't fair, that's all. Damn it, there ought to be another suitable choice." Again, she sighed deeply, and shrugged, as if to shake off the blues and regain her sense of humor.

Nedha winked and smiled as she bent forward to whisper into Mrs. Fenley's ear, something she had never revealed to another soul on the asteroid.

"Why, Mrs. Fenley, on Geyseria, women do have such a choice..."

Straightening up, Nedha proceeded to continue arranging Mrs. Fenley's hair. "Now, what should we do about your bangs? Hmm, curl them under or maybe..."

Gina was no longer paying attention. The soon to be ex-Mrs. Fenley was already plotting and planning a post-divorce vacation to a very private planet.

Her mood was much improved.

Titles By J Lee Bagan

Building the Dream

By Alinar Den

Copyright © 2024 Alinar Den

All rights reserved.

Building the Dream

a short story by Alinar Den

ALINAR DEN

12

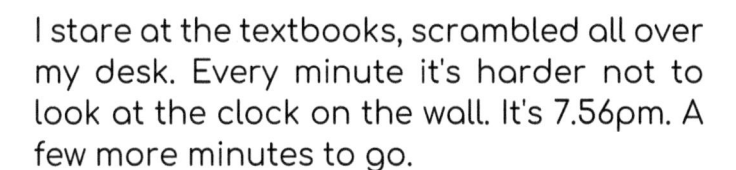

I stare at the textbooks, scrambled all over my desk. Every minute it's harder not to look at the clock on the wall. It's 7.56pm. A few more minutes to go.

It's Saturday, the day when other kids are outdoors or playing video games, or browsing social media... or whatever normal teenagers are doing. They're normal and there is me, studying. I clench my teeth. I shouldn't think this way, it's distracting. I should use every minute to be productive, to invest in my future. I stare at the vocabulary in front of me. All those words and expressions I tried to squeeze in my brain today, all those unfamiliar letters I repeatedly wrote down, they are not staying there. I sigh. My brain is wired differently, that's not how I learn. I wish Mom could understand it.

The quiet alarm dings on my phone. It has just enough volume to not be heard by anyone else and to bring the brightest smile on my face. I keep grinning while slowly removing textbooks from my desk, tucking them in the drawer. It's done. I'm free for today. Mom hasn't checked on me lately. I have her trust. She knows that I will do my best to study, that I will use every minute, trying to squeeze knowledge into my head. Every minute to build a dream. Her dream.

I love 8pm. It's my favorite number and it's the agreed time. Coincidence? Well, probably. The agreement is, at 8pm every day, I belong to myself. I can do anything I want... As long as it's not disturbing my family or neighbors. 8pm is the time when I can spread my wings and fly in the limited space of my bedroom. Actually, I can go out, but this option is never tempting. This time is too precious to waste it on fresh air and communicating with potential real-life friends.

I pull the box from the corner, where it stands hidden all day. The room is lighting up. Not only because the box is filled with colorful objects, I swear I see it glowing, spreading the magical dust.

I look at Fluffy curling on my bed, he looks back with interest. Of course. The moment I start pulling my stuff out of the box, it's going to become his playground for the rest of the day.

Mom was right when she suggested that I should keep the box tucked in the corner during the day. It's distracting. I can't think of anything else when I'm looking at it. Making an obvious choice, I pull out the notebook. It has a lock on it, the type you can break only by looking at it, but it matched the vibe of secrecy, that's why I got it. I open it and cringe immediately. One of the pages shows my latest effort at drawing myself, holding a book. Well, if it was meant to be a self-portrait, it would never be recognized. The shapes and angles are very wrong, it looks like a 2-year-old drew it. I sigh.

Mom says, drawing is not important, that it will never help me reach the dream. That's why I was never in any of the drawing classes, that's why she does her best to help me with school assignments, drawing most of them herself, so I don't have to waste my time, my precious time, on learning how to draw. My teachers proudly display "my drawings" in the class and I can't even look at them. Only me and mom know that the most I did there was blurry backgrounds and silhouettes... Set the foundation, that's what I had to do during the lesson, knowing that mom would take her time correcting my clumsy efforts back at home.

I pull the pen from the box. Sketching with a pen might not be my smartest idea, but I hate pencils. The way they sound, the chances they give. Maybe I don't want a second chance, maybe I don't want to erase the messiness and start over, maybe I'm just crazy. I draw a line in the notebook and I know immediately that I'm going to mess it up and it will be as ugly as my drawings usually are. I know it but I continue, feeling sweat building up on my forehead. It takes a lot of mental energy not to stop, not to hate it, not to start crossing out everything, not to throw this innocent notebook at the wall.

I briefly look at the box and Fluffy, who's trying to pull something out of it. The guitar is the most obvious item in the box. The instrument that scares the shit out of me. The farthest I got with it was holding it in my hands. I know that one day I will be ready. One day... I sigh.

Music was also labeled as the least important part of my life.

"Why do you need it? Will playing a guitar give you a chance in life... money or fame? It's good only to entertain your friends around the campfire." Mom said once, and I believed her. And she was right, because listening to me singing will never make anyone happy. No talent, just passion. The story of my life.

I keep drawing until I feel it's done and put the notebook away, in the bottom of the box. My mind is wondering, not knowing what to do next. So many choices, so little time...

22

"I had to..." I'm writing down in my diary, my feelings ready to overflow.

I'm sitting on the couch in my cozy living room. The TV is not on, it rarely is. A plate with a half-eaten dinner is sitting on the coffee table. I'm not feeling hungry, I rarely do when I'm stressed. It's 8.30pm and it makes me smile. Weird habits are weird. I still can't let it go; I can only become myself after 8pm.

"I had to..." I repeat to myself, confirming what I just wrote, but it still doesn't feel like the truth.

My mom said that it's not a good idea to keep serving in the restaurant after I graduate. It was a good idea while I was studying, because it gave me financial independence and it helped with getting my introvertive ass out of its shell. But it was not a good fit for me anymore, because I was supposed to be as ambitious as all the other people with a master's degree. She said that I had to find the job that fits, that will help me not only get my bills paid, but help me to strategically build the dream... Her dream.

Of course, I agreed and found the job. I had spent so many years training for it that it wasn't complicated. I pretended to be passionate about forms and numbers, about the stability of office life and career growth. They believed me. Of course they did.

It's been a couple of months of me wearing a suit and following the business crowd flow. I'm a good worker, that's what both my boss and mom say to me. I'm not sure where she gets the information from, but she seems pretty confident about it. I have a public transport monthly pass now, though I barely use it because I prefer walking to work. I have my favorite drink in the nearest coffee shop and the baristas smile at me a lot because I tip well... I have a lot of boring clothes that I hate with all my soul, but have to wear every day.

I just miss my friends. My old restaurant team became a family to me and the moment I quit, I chipped off, breaking their hearts and my own. There was no way back, there was no US anymore and we all knew it.

"I had to..." I repeated the phrase I wrote; it was being smudged now by my flowing tears.

I looked at the walk-in closet door. The box was there and I still pulled it out every day, but it wasn't glowing anymore, lighting the room. There were not many things I truly enjoyed now. I brushed my hands through the familiar colorful pieces and pulled my tablet out. It was so much easier to draw on it than it was in my old notebooks. Technologies... It still wasn't pretty or professional, but it was me.

I opened my last drawing, holding a stylus pen in the air, not knowing what to do about the mess in front of me. Just a background and silhouettes. Weirdly enough, it made me smile. Mom wasn't going to fix this one for me, not this time, not in the foreseeable future. She hasn't seen my drawings since I finished school. Not like there was something special to see, not like there was something to salvage.

32

"Do you play?"

The guitar is standing next to the TV and it is too obvious, it's a statement now, filling my living room with its glow.

"Not professionally." I offer a shy smile.

It's our fifth date and we know each other well enough to spend it at my place. The awkward silence is chasing us, but we're working through it with the traditional date conversations.

I would say more about my guitar to fill the gaps, but I'm not ready to admit that I started playing it only a few years ago, though I have had it since I was 10... and that it's not still tucked in the box in the closet only because there is no box left anymore. I briefly look at the drawing tablet, freely standing on my desk next to the clock. 6:15pm is showing in huge digits. I smile.

I clear my throat and add quietly:

"I play in one bar on the weekends..."

"Really?" The surprise is obvious and I note the admiration and maybe a tiny bit of jealousy. "I thought you were teaching classes on the weekend."

I smile again, remembering the last time I handed over the happy kids, almost fully covered in paint, back to their proud parents. I also handed the kids framed artworks to their family members. Framing was important, to show them that, though the drawings are weird and mostly ugly, they were complete.

"In the daytime." I croak, feeling the blush in my cheeks.

The silence covers us again, but I don't mind it at all.

I prefer not to say many things about myself. I enjoy the looks on people's faces when I tell them about the time I spend building the dream... MY dream.

Titles By Alinar Den

Titles By JJ Caler

The Carrigan Chronicles

Lia's Odyssey

Coffee and Dreams

ABOUT THE AUTHOR

You can't make us talk.